The Wonderful Tree

The Wonderful Tree

A STORY OF THE SEASONS

Text by Adelaide Holl from a story by György Lehoczky

Paintings by György Lehoczky

Golden Press, New York • Western Publishing Company, Inc., Racine, Wisconsin

Second Printing, 1975

It was autumn. A chill wind blew across the yellowing fields. In the orchard, the long ladders of the fruit pickers still leaned against the branches. A few golden pears hung among the golden leaves, but most of the ripe fruit had been harvested and stored before the coming of frost.

The summer birds were gone. Only an occasional straggler hovered over the stubble and in the orchard, gathering bits of scattered grain and over-ripe fruit.

Except for a few lingering wild asters, the field flowers had withered and dried. Where there had once been blossoms and leaves, there were now little gray seed pods on parched and brittle stalks.

The skies had a streaked and wintry look, and there was a hint of frost in the air.

But indoors it was snug and cozy. A fire burned cheerfully inside Grandfather's tiled stove, casting a mellow glow over the brightly painted cupboard against the wall. On the ledge by the hot stove, Grandfather had placed apples for roasting, and now they sputtered and sizzled and scented the whole room with their pungent fragrance.

Christopher bit deep into a warm apple. It was tangy and delicious. Grandfather pointed to the little brown seeds inside the fruit. "See, Chris," he said, "if you plant one of these seeds in the earth, it will one day grow into an apple tree. And each apple on that tree will have within it more little brown seeds to make more apple trees."

"How does a seed know that it should grow into an apple tree, or a pear tree, or a plum tree?" Christopher asked. "What if I planted an apple seed and it grew into a pear tree?"

Grandfather smiled. "There are no mistakes in nature," he said. "Each seed, each bud, each living creature has its own special place in nature's design. The little birds know when to fly south as summer wanes, and they need no map to chart their flight. The spider knows by instinct how to spin her silken thread. The honeybee knows exactly how to fashion the wax cells of the honeycomb and how to fill them with nectar from the meadow flowers. And an apple seed will always grow into an apple tree; a pear seed will always grow into a pear tree."

The sound of thunder came from far off like the slow, measured rolling of drums.

"Nature is getting ready for winter," Grandfather said. "She will sweep away the few golden leaves that still cling to the trees. She will wash the branches clean. She will deck the orchards and woods with white lace and spread a white coverlet over the earth and its sleeping creatures.

"But come now," he added, "it is late. It is time we, too, were sleeping."

For a long time Christopher lay in bed listening to the howling of the storm outside. The rain pounded on the roof. The wind rattled against the shutters on the windows and whistled down the chimney.

"The wind is playing a flute in the stove," thought Christopher, "and the raindrops are beating time to the music."

He fell asleep at last and dreamed that he was alone in the dark, stormy night, struggling against the savage wind, hurrying toward the warmth of Grandfather's house. When he reached the door and pushed it open, the whole place had been miraculously transformed into an orchard. All the apples and pears in Grandfather's cupboard had sprouted and grown into hundreds of trees weighted down with ripe fruit. Suddenly there was a flurry of wings, and a great flock of birds flew in and picked the branches clean.

Christopher woke with a start. It was daylight. The wind and the rain had stopped, and there was a curious stillness over everything. He ran to the window. The whole world seemed to have changed color overnight.

The blue skies of autumn had changed to the gray skies of winter. The trees had been stripped of their rust and gold and now stood bleakly outlined against the sky. The meadows and hills, the house roofs and fence posts were all shrouded in white. On the branches of the pear tree outside the window, a few bedraggled birds huddled against the cold.

Christopher ran downstairs. "Grandfather," he shouted, "look at the snow! After breakfast, I can get out the sled and go coasting on the hill!"

"It's a splendid day for coasting," agreed Grandfather. "And for sleigh riding. When I was a boy, we had a wonderful sleigh and four wonderful horses. We hitched the team to the sleigh and went racing over the frozen ground with the harness bells jingling and the snow crunching under the sleigh runners."

"Wasn't it cold?" asked Christopher.

"Very cold," replied Grandfather. "Our breath made little steamy clouds in the winter air, and sometimes tiny icicles froze on our eyelashes. But we filled our pockets with hot roasted chestnuts to warm our hands, and we heated bricks in the fireplace and wrapped them in blankets to warm our feet. We bundled ourselves in layers of coats, and sweaters, and robes. It was great fun!

"We were even colder walking to church," Grandfather continued, "but that was fun, too. We looked for the tracks of foxes, and rabbits, and deer. We looked for the delicate star-prints of winter birds in the snow. We stuffed our pockets with bits of grain and kernels of corn to scatter about for the wild creatures.

"Winter seemed to bring man and beast closer together. The birds would come into the village to take shelter in the warm stables and under the snow-covered roofs. The deer would come down out of the hills to browse near the houses. The foxes foraged in our corncribs, and the squirrels, like little bandits, stole nuts from our attics. We never forgot the wild things in winter, especially at Christmastime. We put out sheaves of grain and chunks of bread and meat to share our holiday feast with them."

Christopher said, "I can't wait till Christmas! I can't wait to put up a tree! Did you have a Christmas tree when you were a boy, Grandfather?"

Grandfather's eyes were bright with remembering. "We brought in a fir tree from the woods," he said, "and we decked it with garlands of popcorn, and cranberries, and tiny wax candles. On Christmas Eve we went caroling through the streets of the village.

"Three boys would don bright cloaks and make shiny tin crowns for their heads and pretend to be the Three Kings of the Orient bearing gifts to the Christ Child. Little girls would put on white veils and tinseled wings to represent the angels who sang at the first Christmas. And there were small shepherds with their shepherds' pipes, like the shepherds of old on the hills of Bethlehem. We lighted our way through the dark with candles, and the villagers would come out of their warm houses to offer us gifts of sweet cakes and candies."

Christopher said, "Sometimes I think winter is my favorite time of the year. When the pond is frozen over, I can go ice skating. I can build snowmen, and race the other boys on my sled. But then," he added, "I love spring, too. In spring I can look for frogs' eggs in the pond, and I can make a kite and fly it."

"I guess spring has always been the most celebrated of seasons," said Grandfather. "Long ago, long before I was a boy, people made a festival of spring. At the renewal of the growing season, everyone rejoiced—the nobles and knights in their great castles, the peasants in their villages, the shepherds in their humble, thatched cottages. They sang, and danced, and decked themselves with spring blossoms, and thanked the angels of heaven for the eternal cycle of seasons, for the end of the old and the beginning of the new."

"But, Grandfather," said Christopher, "why would people celebrate spring more than the other seasons?"

"In days of old," Grandfather went on, "people had to grow all their own food, produce their wool for clothing, and gather in a supply of fuel for the winter. Sometimes when supplies were low, the winter months were cold and dark, times of hunger and hardship. Spring meant the return of the warm sun, the return of birds, the thawing of frozen streams. In spring there were newborn lambs in the fold, new colts in the pasture, and new fawns in the forest. There were fresh eggs in the henhouse and newly hatched baby chicks. There were newborn calves in the barnyard and fresh, sweet grass to make fresh, sweet milk. There were blossoms on the fruit trees and green shoots pushing up out of the earth in the garden."

Christopher listened intently. "I'm not sure I have a favorite season," he said, "but summer is lots of fun. School is out, and I can walk barefoot in the grass. I can swim, and fish, and go on picnics. Sometimes I think that summer doesn't last long enough."

Grandfather chuckled. "Summer, like all the other seasons, is just exactly long enough to carry out nature's plan. It is long enough for the birds to nest, hatch their eggs, and send the nestlings off on their own wings. It is long enough for the wiggly caterpillar to spin its cradle, grow its wings, and turn into a butterfly. It is long enough for the summer flowers to bloom, then to drop their petals and produce new seeds for another year. It is just long enough for the trees in the orchard to curl their blossoms and repeat the miracle of the fruit. There is a rhythm, a perfect timing in the scheme of things. Nature needs no calendar."

Christopher nodded. "Yes," he agreed, "and after summer it will always be autumn again. That is nature's plan, isn't it?"

He glanced at the pear tree outside the window. "Grandfather," he said, "now the pear tree is bare, but if I close my eyes, I can see it as it looks in all four seasons. I can see it covered with pink blossoms in spring. I can see it leafy and green with summer birds nesting in its branches. I can see it with ripe pears in autumn. And I can see it as it is now, leafless, and quiet, and resting."

Grandfather smiled. "The whole world is a miracle of order, of perfect harmony. And now that you have discovered it as a boy, Chris, you will not forget it when you are a man."

Grandfather stood up. He placed some bricks on the stove. "Now I have a surprise for you," he said. "There is a man in the village who has horses and a sleigh. He is going to let us borrow them. So dress yourself warmly, and get some robes and blankets. We will take a sleigh ride just like the kind I took when I was a boy."

Christopher beamed. "Oh, Grandfather, that will be fun! Can we take some corn and grain with us to feed the birds and the squirrels?"

"Of course," said Grandfather. "Our little friends in the woods will be glad to see us. They have to search hard to find food when the ground is covered with snow."

He put his hand on Christopher's shoulder. "Come, let us get ready," he said.